I Love You Because You're You

by Liza Baker

Illustrated by
David McPhail

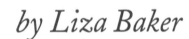

SCHOLASTIC INC. Cartwheel BOOKS ®

New York Toronto London Auckland Sydney
Mexico City New Delhi Hong Kong Buenos Aires

ISBN-13: 978-0-545-11777-7
ISBN-10: 0-545-11777-1

12 11 10 9 8 7 6 5 4 3 2 1   8 9 10 11 12 13/0

Printed in the U.S.A.   23

This edition first printing, October 2008

For Jenny and Mom & Dad — for your inspiration
— L.B.

For David's new best friend, McKenzie
— D.M.

I love you when you're happy
and grinning ear to ear.

I love you when you're sleepy
and want to snuggle near.

I love you when you're silly
and dancing 'round
and 'round.

I love you when you're frightened
and hear a scary sound.

I love you when you're bashful
and hide behind my knee.

I love you when you're brave,
and from my arms you flee.

I love you when you're curious
and searching here and there.

I love you when you're proud,
your head held in the air.

I love you when you're sick
and need to rest in bed.

I love you when you're frisky
and standing on your head.

I love you when you're sad
and need a kiss and hug.

I love you when you're playful
and rolling on the rug.

I love you when you're angry
and cross your arms and pout.

I love you when you're wild
and yell and scream and shout.

I love you
any way you feel,
no matter
what you do.

I love you
any way you are.

I love you
because
you're you!